Fort Wayne, Indiana 46808

FRIEN
OF ACPL

W9-BNZ-667

The Fire-Brother

KEVIN CROSSLEY-HOLLAND
The Fire-Brother

Illustrated by
JOANNA TROUGHTON

A Clarion Book
THE SEABURY PRESS
NEW YORK

First American edition 1975
Text copyright © 1974 by Kevin Crossley-Holland
Illustrations copyright © 1974 by William Heinemann Ltd
Library of Congress Catalog Card Number: 74-24764
ISBN: 0-8164-3143-4

All rights reserved.
No part of this book may be reproduced in any form,
except for brief extracts in reviews,
without the written permission of the publisher.

Printed in Great Britain

L 2119579

for Kieran and Dominic

O Almighty God, who willest to be glorified in thy Saints and didst raise up thy servants Cedd and the Saints of Essex to shine as lights in the world: Shine we pray thee, in our hearts, that we also in our generation may show forth thy praises who hast called us out of darkness into thy marvellous light; through Jesus Christ our Lord. Amen.

"Go away!" said Oswald desperately. As if he were alone on the common land with a dark-eyed bull, and couldn't control it. "Go away! Go away!"

But Wulf stood his ground, looking down on his elder brother who sprawled against the south wall of their hut. It hurt to hear the bitter words, but it would have hurt even more to go.

"Go away!" shouted Oswald, sitting up now, tense and angry. "What good are you to us, or to anyone in Ythancestir?"

"We, well we've built . . ."

". . . What good is your fine new monastery to us?" said Oswald. "Tell me that."

Wulf's mind stammered. He knew that there were answers, good answers. If only he could think he would find the words.

"Go on!" said Oswald. "Preach a sermon at me. That's the only reason you come here each evening."

"No, no," said Wulf.

"To warn against our ways, to give us promises and more promises, always about heaven and Christ, and . . ."

"Christ!" snorted Wulf's mother. She had dozed off in the hot burst of sunlight that followed the rain of that August afternoon but now Oswald's voice roused her. "Christ!" she said again. "You and your Christian monks are free enough with your promises of heaven. But, Wulf, what are you going to do about now?"

"Now doesn't matter most," said Wulf. "Now is soon yesterday."

"What do you mean?" said his mother. "What are we going

to do this winter, with this terrible harvest, all the corn beaten flat by wind and by rain? If we'd sacrificed to Freya, as we used to do, instead of praying to Christ. . . ."

Oswald gave Wulf no chance to reply. "And if the King had not given a hide of our land to the northern monks." He shook his head. "*I'm* not your brother. The monks are your brothers. Cedd the Bishop is your father."

Wulf looked at his mother, then at Oswald. "I only come here because I want to come," he said. "You're my mother, my brother. Anna's my sister."

"Leave him alone," said Wulf's mother before Oswald could bully him further. Then she turned to her younger son. "Wulf, why don't you come home? Things aren't going well for the Christians, but they're not going well for us either. And this is where you belong."

Wulf turned away quickly to hide the tears that started to his eyes, quite without warning. He knew his only home now was with Cedd, and with the monks. And as he hurried from the hut, Anna darted out of it. In there, she'd tried to hide from the endless quarrelling. Now she simply grabbed Wulf's wrist and half-hung on it, slowing him.

Wulf squeezed her left hand and held on to it as they walked past the straggle of small huts and out of the hamlet. They paddled through every puddle on the pocked track.

"I'm five tomorrow," Anna said.

"I know," said Wulf.

"I can't wait," Anna said. "Can you wait till I'm five?"

"No," said Wulf, smiling.

"I can't either," said Anna.

"I've made something for you," said Wulf.

"What thing?" Anna asked.

"Something," said Wulf.

Then Anna ran back to her mother and Oswald. Her fair hair jumped up and down on her head as she went. And Wulf took the way out of Ythancestir towards the church and the monastery and the endless sea. He could not help but think about the meetings with his mother and Oswald which daily became more bitter, each time with more accusations levelled at Cedd and the monks. I must tell Cedd what my mother said about the harvest, he thought, and what Oswald said about the Christians giving nothing but promises. If only I'd found the right answers.

As Wulf drew near to the great stone church, surrounded by the wooden huts where the monks worked and ate and slept, he heard the bell announce the service of Compline. Five minutes, thought Wulf. He quickened his step then, and left behind him that hurtful hour in Ythancestir.

Wulf hurried to the boys' end of the monks' dormitory, and there his friends, sons of men in Ythancestir, greeted him.

"Quiet!" said an old monk, very firmly. "You know the rule. Silence when the bell begins to toll."

"You're the cantor tonight," whispered Edwin who, like Wulf, was twelve.

"Aidan aid me!" said Wulf. "I'd forgotten."

"I hope you haven't forgotten the psalm," said Edwin.

"Quiet!" said the old monk.

Wulf grinned at Edwin.

In ones and twos and small knots all the monks in the monastery at Ythancestir, sixty of them and five boys beside Wulf, made their way to the church. Outside, the day's colours were failing: the sky over the sea was lumpy, a thick purplish grey; and over Ythancestir, in the west, it was streaky lilac and pewter and palest blue. Inside the church it was at once darker and brighter. The walls were shadowy and the lofty roof was shadowy, but the twin altar candles seemed to have set fire to the great gold crucifix between them. And the corona of candles near by, standing on a pedestal, selected the gold strands in the altar cloth and singled out the gold cross of the man waiting in front of the altar, Cedd, Bishop of the East Saxons, Abbot of Ythancestir.

Cedd saw Wulf come in and indicated that, as cantor, he should stand at his left side. Then the shuffling stopped. A stillness grew out of the place. The monks' faces looked white in the dim light. The church smelt of honey.

"May t' Lord Almighty grant us a quiet night," said Cedd, "and a perfect end." Cedd's calm, strong voice seemed to Wulf to be saying more than it actually said. "Brothers," said the Bishop, "be loving, be alert. Your enemy, t' devil, goes abaht in many disguises. . . ."

Wulf was filled with a great comforting warmth. His mind wandered back to that spring morning fifteen months before when Cedd baptised him on the same spot where the church now stood, amongst the ruins of the old Roman fort. He could hear Cedd saying, "Wulf, Wulf, I knew thou'd want to fight for Christ. To lead a fair life, a kind life, trying to love thy enemies, slow to anger, quick to forgive." Then Wulf thought of Oswald and his mother, how he did love them, how somehow he couldn't explain to them.

"Glory be to t' Father," said Cedd, "and to t' Son: and to t' Holy Ghost."

Then as the monks responded with one voice, he bent to Wulf and whispered, "It's thee now."

Wulf nodded; his heart thumped. And as the reverberation of the monks' voices died away he drew in his breath and began to chant in his clear treble voice:

O praise the Lord of heaven: praise him in the height.
Praise him, sun and moon: praise him, all ye stars and light.
Praise the Lord upon earth: ye dragons and all deeps.

12

Wulf sang well, balancing the two halves of each verse, articulating each word carefully. He was quite dry-mouthed as he finished his great psalm of praise and Cedd resumed, praising God, promising the monks, "T' parched ground'll become a pool, and t' thirsty land springs of water: in t' habitation of dragons, where each lay, shall be grass, with reeds and rushes."

Dragons, thought Wulf. Always dragons.

The short service of Compline ended. Cedd prayed for peace in the silent hours of the night and Wulf walked out into the cool darkness.

A strict rule of silence was observed now, and the monks and boys together filed back to the dormitory; their sandals flapped against the wooden boards. Wulf was soon in bed; and, in bed, soon asleep. The day's work, the hurtful argument, the responsibility as cantor, had worn him out.

Wulf was restless that night. He moaned a little in his sleep. He turned his head from side to side as if he were trying to escape his own thoughts. Then he began to dream. He was alone in the church with Cedd and he dreamed Cedd was telling him that he must fight the enemy in the woods behind Ythancestir. Then all the monks rushed in and pressed on him a helmet, shouting "This is the helmet of salvation," and a shield, shouting "This is the shield of faith" and a huge gleaming sword, shouting "This is the sword of the spirit." Then Wulf dreamed that he went on his way alone. The woods were dark, and the sun—the sky's great candle—only burst through the foliage here and there. He kept tripping. His right

elbow ached and he wondered whether he would be able to
carry and wield the great sword. So he came to an open place,
a glade. At its end was a mound and it was there, his enemy.
It breathed fire and smoke. And though he could not see it,
he could hear it ranting and roaring, and it kept shouting
something, the same thing, something he could not quite make
out, in a voice he thought he recognized. Wulf wanted to run
away, yet thought he had to stay, for some reason to stay. . . .

Wulf woke, damp with sweat and terrified. Round him he
heard heavy breathing and snoring. He realized where he was;
in bed, in the dormitory, his friends around him. Even so, he
felt afraid.

Then the monastery bell began to toll. "Nocturns," Wulf
whispered to himself. "Seven times a day do I praise thee. At

midnight I will rise and give thanks to thee."

The monks stirred, slipped on their tunics and gowns by the dim light of the single great beeswax candle, and padded away to the church. The boys were excused this one service on the grounds that it was not wise that they should break their night's sleep. But Wulf was glad to rise now, to get away from his nightmare. He dressed quickly and hurried to the church.

Cedd was waiting in that silent, friendly place. He saw Wulf, half-raised his eyebrows, half-smiled.

Once more, after sleep and before sleep, the monks praised their Maker and prayed for the dove of peace.

It was a brilliant morning. There had been more rain during the night, and now the sun exploited it, using each puddle and wet surface as a reflector. A cool wind blew in off the sea.

Wulf was glad to get out of the dim refectory into the bright light, the more so as there were only a few minutes before the start of Brother Patrick's morning classes. He walked through the enclosure surrounded by the long huts and out of the great gate in the east wall. Unlike the rest of the old fort which had been raided for the construction of the church, this wall had been left intact as a windbreak between the sea and the monastery.

"Cedd!" said Wulf, surprised and delighted.

Cedd looked up from the jetty steps where he was sitting and grinned, as if he and Wulf were conspirators who had

found a way of being alone.

"I mean . . ."

"Thou means, what am I doing here," said Cedd. "The same as thee, Wulf." He stretched out his arms as if he meant to pull down the sun out of the sky.

"I wanted to see you," said Wulf.

"I don't see thee as often as I might," said Cedd, shaking his head.

Wulf shook his head too. "I can understand that," he said. "You've sixty sons here now."

"Thou'rt chiding me," said Cedd. And then, sudden and direct and concerned as ever, he asked, "What ails thee, Wulf?"

Wulf looked past Cedd out to the sea. "My mother," he said. "And Oswald. They ail me. They're against me, and I don't know what to do, or think, or say. Every evening, when I visit them, they complain about the monks here and about Christ Himself, and they curse the day you came and . . ."

"Aye," said Cedd, raising a hand to restrain Wulf's torrent of words, then thinking better of it and letting him go on.

So Wulf did go on, and told Cedd how each meeting seemed worse than the last, no matter what he said or if he said nothing, and asked why it should be so, and how he should answer them.

"All thou sayest saddens me," said Cedd. "But nothing surprises me. Thy mother and brother love thee well enough. It's not just thee on one side and them on t' other. I'll tell thee this: all t' people of Ythancestir are unhappy; their ungrateful mouths are full of complaints and curses."

"But why?" asked Wulf. "And what's it got to do with us?"

"This evening," said Cedd, "I have to see t' Earl Athulf. We can walk together to Ythancestir, thee and I. And after I've seen him, I'll be able to give thee a better answer."

Wulf nodded, and looked worried.

"Think!" said Cedd. "T' people of your place were quick to accept t' word of Christ. 'Appen all too quick." He paused, and spoke as if he was thinking aloud. "Tell me, when have t' old folk ever really liked anything new? Hast heard St. Matthew's saying, 'Neither do men put new wine into old bottles'? That's true, is that. Perhaps the first real Christians are those that grow up so; like you and Edwin and t' other lads here; like me in Northumbria, thirty years ago."

"You're disappointed," said Wulf, frowning, feeling his own family and friends were to blame.

Cedd laughed, and ran his right hand through his short black hair. "No, lad, not disappointed. But impatient. I am that: impatient. Anyroad, let thy mother and Oswald not ail thee. Restrain thy tongue from rough words, thy hand from blows, and thy mind from all harsh thoughts of them. That's not easy."

"No," said Wulf.

"Nothing is ever easy in t' kingdom of earth," said Cedd, smiling. "Go now, or thou'll be late for Brother Patrick's classes. May t' warm eye of Christ shine upon thee."

Then Wulf ran back through the cloisters to the little class-room which was next to the library. For a moment he stood outside the door and listened. The first subject of the morning, Latin grammar, was already begun.

"How many genders of nouns are there at all?" he heard Brother Patrick saying.

"Four." That was Edwin. Or was it Edmund?

"What are they?"

"The first is masculine, as in *hic magister*."

"What is the second?"

"Feminine, as in *haec musa*. And the third is . . ."

"Wait until I ask you," said Brother Patrick.

Wulf glanced over his shoulder at the cloisters, at the roof of the church that seemed to smoulder as the sun dried it, and then he walked into the classroom.

"Wulf," said Brother Patrick, without waiting for any explanations. "How many persons of pronouns are there?"

"Three, Brother Patrick."

"What are they?"

"The first is *ego*."

"And the second . . . ?"

"Is *tu*."

"And the third?"

"The third is *ille*," said Wulf.

"Very good. What is the Latin for late?"

"I . . . I don't know."

"*Tardus*. Why *are* you late?"

"I was talking to Cedd, Brother Patrick."

"What kind of a Bishop is it at all," said Brother Patrick, "that keeps a boy from his classes? And what kind of a monk

will you be without knowing
your declensions and cases
and conjugations? Can you tell me
that?"

Wulf smiled.

The hours passed with an
arithmetic class and a class in
which the six boys practised
their writing, each with a
stylus and a wax tablet. So
the morning ended, and
five minutes before midday
the bell began to toll for the
office of Prime.

"God help you," said Brother
Patrick, and dismissed the
class with a wave of his small fat
hand. "I doubt if I can."

The boys hurried then
from the classroom to the
church. Wulf could see Oswald
pacing up and down on his
strip of land which was the
nearest to that land belonging
to the monastery. He raised his
hand to his brother as he had
done each day throughout
the summer.

Oswald did not wave back. He didn't turn away. He simply stood motionless and watched as Wulf slowly and forlornly let his arm fall and was surrounded then by a tide of black monks who carried him forward into the church.

After Prime the monks gathered in the refectory for the main meal of the day and, as usual, it was the duty of the boys to carry in the food and set it before the monks—hunks of meat from a freshly slaughtered pig; apples tempting to look at and touch and smell, let alone to taste; and bowls of pale milk from which the cream had been skimmed to make butter and cheese. The monks ate noisily, but in silence, listening or pretending to listen as an old monk read some verses from St Mark's Gospel.

Wulf didn't mind running to and fro with the monks' food before eating his own meal; he didn't mind the rule of silence. Outside these walls, he thought sometimes, people can be against us, they can be against each other, but here in this monastery so little changes; it's the same pattern from day to day. There was something reassuring about that.

So it was that after the midday meal Wulf went, as he always did, to the monastery workshop to carve bone with the old monk, Brother Edward. This workshop was a shed that leaned against the north-east corner of the old fortress; it had no front to it, so the light from the south and west streamed into it. In effect it was no more than a canopy to keep out the rain, an arbour to welcome the sun—in fact, an ideal place for craftsmen. Here the stones used for building the new church had been squared; here the grave headstone for Brother

Ceorl who died the previous autumn from an adder's bite had been hewn and incised with a cross; here Brother Edward hammered out silver Saulus and Paulus spoons like those Cedd had given to Wulf when he first came to Ythancestir and then returned and christened Wulf; and here the gold chalice that was used in the church had been carefully moulded and decorated with a marvellous design—an interweaving of ribbons that seemed to Wulf to have no beginning and no end.

This was the part of the day Wulf liked best. He was carving a little casket out of whalebone, and incising a cross on each side of it. And he was cutting the face of a man on the lid. Brother Edward had promised him that, if it were well done, it could house some relic—perhaps even a piece of St Aidan's mantle—and be placed in the sacrarium in the church. Wulf had been working at it all summer and he thought that, as like as not, it would take him until winter to finish it. Day by day he chipped at it, left it, returned to it; it was growing. Sometimes he thought the face on the lid had a sort of life of its own and stood back and looked at it, amazed, as if he were seeing it for the first time. At other times, when his chisel slipped and he chipped away a flake of bone by mistake, he was upset at his own carelessness; he would rather have cut himself.

Brother Edward saw that Wulf had a great gift for carving and mostly left him alone. Wulf was grateful for that and he knew that whenever he wanted it, Brother Edward would give him advice and reassurance.

So the two of them, the twelve-year-old boy and the old

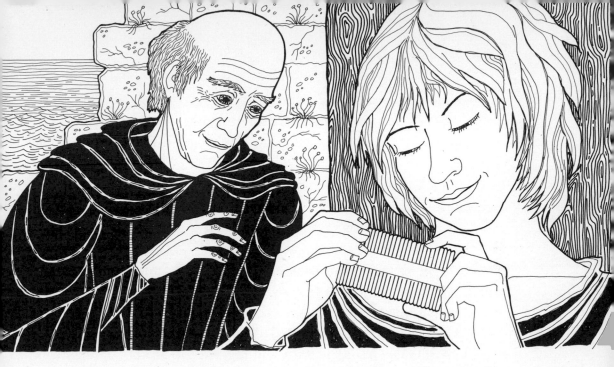

man, worked together in companionable silence through the heat of the afternoon. From time to time Brother Edward took a look at the length of the shadows about them, and said at last, "Ten minutes, Wulf."

"Ten," said Wulf, startled. "Only ten."

"You should stop now. Don't forget . . ."

"I haven't," said Wulf quickly. He put the casket away in the wooden chest at the back of the arbour. Then dipped his hand into his tunic and brought out a small, perfectly-cut bone comb.

"Lovely," said Brother Edward appreciatively.

Wulf laid the comb on the trestle table, placed his finger-tips over one end, and then with a stylus lightly inscribed four letters on the bar between the upper and lower teeth.

"It's a fair name," said Brother Edward.

Wulf narrowed his eyes, rubbed at the last letter with the sleeve of his tunic and then inscribed it again.

"You have them straight," said Brother Edward. "Five minutes."

Wulf took a metal spike and scratched the ivory where he had marked it, at first delicately, and then with firmer strokes. The bone powdered and Wulf kept blowing it away.

"There," he said. "I've done it."

"It's well done," said Brother Edward. He put an arm round Wulf's shoulders. And almost at once the bell began to spell out the minutes before Nones.

After the monks had celebrated the ninth hour, it was time for Wulf to take his turn with milling the flour and, later, rounding up and milking the cows. And while he was occupied in these ways, the other boys and the sixty monks were all at their own appointed duties—one on the monastery land, gathering a sackful of cabbages and one in the steamy kitchen, already preparing the evening meal for the monks; one shoeing a horse and one sawing wood for a new table in the refectory; one scraping calfskin, removing the blemishes, preparing the hide for use in the scriptorium, and one in the scriptorium itself, illuminating a copy of the Gospels with endless patience and brilliant colours, gold foil, green dye, saffron, and purple dye made from crushed lapis lazuli; one alone in the church decorating the plaster in the apse with a painting of Christ ascending to heaven; and many a one besides out on the road or in near-by villages, taking medicine to those who were sick, teaching and preaching about Christ to those who still believed in the heathen gods. Wherever they went, they tried to leave men happier and more hopeful because of their coming. Only eighteen months after the cornerstone had been laid, the monastery of Ythancestir, humming with activity like a great hive, supported itself and gave sweetness to others.

Early that evening, after Vespers and the light meal that followed it, Cedd and Wulf took the straight sandy path that led to Ythancestir. Ahead of them they could see Edmund, Wulf's closest friend, already hurrying to see his own mother and father. And, as they went, they met several brothers returning late from the more distant hamlets.

"It's a sour summer, is this," said Cedd.

Wulf tugged at a blade of grass, unsheathed it, and stuck the sweet, succulent root between his teeth.

"Think on this morning," said Cedd, "and look at t' sky now."

"They're anxious almost," said Wulf, staring at the clouds racing inland.

"They're chasing t' sun," said Cedd. "Wolf-clouds, chasing t' sun." He rubbed his lips together. "And look at t' corn, lad. If t' people are unhappy, it's nowt to wonder at."

Either side of the path the patches of corn lay wrecked, half-flattened, a miserable sight.

"'Appen there'll be enough," said Cedd. "It's bad for them and bad for us. But we'll scavenge and glean and so get past."

As they neared Ythancestir, Wulf dragged his feet, thinking of the meeting ahead; and then he asked Cedd if he would come with him to see his mother and Oswald and Anna. But at once he felt a coward and wished he hadn't. Cedd knew that. "Each of us to our own fight," he said slowly, shaking his head. "I'll come onetime, Wulf, but not tonight." He smiled at Wulf. "Remember what I told thee this morning," he said, and he turned towards Earl Athulf's hall.

A moment later Anna ran out of the hut to greet her brother and they embraced. Then without more ado Wulf pulled the bone comb out of his tunic pocket and tugged it through Anna's hair.

She yelped, and grabbed the comb, and inspected it.

"It's for you," said Wulf. "I made it."

That made Anna happy in a way she couldn't explain. "I'm five," she said joyfully.

"I know."

"Could you wait?"

"No, I couldn't wait," said Wulf, grinning.

"I'll wear it," said Anna, sticking the comb back into her hair.

"It'll fall out," said Wulf. "Look!" And he showed Anna her name incised on the flat rib between the two sets of teeth.

"I'm going to show Oswald," said Anna, and she hared back towards the hut, ahead of Wulf.

Oswald was standing in front of the entrance as if he were defending it. He took no notice at all of Anna who tugged at his sleeve but, as Wulf drew near, he spat deliberately in front of him.

Wulf's heart pumped uncomfortably.

"Go away!" said Oswald in a low voice.

That scared Anna and she ran away to find her mother and show her the comb that Wulf had made for her.

Wulf forced himself to look at his brother and saw that his eyes were blazing.

"You've moved my markers," said Oswald.

"What?" said Wulf, astonished.

"You heard. You've moved my markers."

"Where?"

"The two nearest the monastery. You've stolen six paces of my land."

"Oswald!" exclaimed Wulf. "How could you?"

Oswald looked at the ground.

"Me!" said Wulf. "Stealing *your* land?"

"Go away!" snarled Oswald.

Then Wulf suddenly remembered his dream of the night before, the journey he did not want to make, the repeated words. Over the forest, away west, the clouds were gathering, and bleeding.

"You," said Oswald. "One of your monks. You've stolen my land. What the monks weren't given by the King, they thieve inch by inch."

"No!" cried Wulf angrily.

"Where will it end?" shouted Oswald.

"It's untrue, untrue," protested Wulf. "You know it is."

Oswald spat again. "Where will it end? You tell us not to make boasts but pray; you tell us not to throw spears but sing psalms; you take our land."

"No monk in the monastery would ever steal land," shouted Wulf, more angry and upset than he had ever been before.

"You and your monks," sneered Oswald. "We'll use our pitchforks. Our swords can sleep. We'll use our forks and pitch you all into the sea."

"Liar!" shouted Wulf. "Oswald! Liar! Liar!" He heard himself shouting louder and louder.

Then, quite suddenly, Oswald turned and slouched off, muttering something. Wulf looked at him, amazed. He had stood firm and Oswald had backed down; it had never been that way before. But Wulf felt no kind of pleasure. All he wanted to do was sob.

That was an end to it. Wulf could barely stay; he didn't want to go, but there was nothing else to do. Without seeing his sister again, and without seeing his mother at all, neither of whom were about, Wulf hurried out of the hamlet back towards the monastery.

As he thought over that violent argument time and again, Wulf felt a pressing pain in his chest. He didn't see how things could ever get better between him and his brother and mother; each meeting seemed, and was, worse than the last. The wind, as if uncertain which way to go, swirled and skirled around him.

"Lighten our darkness," cried Cedd. "And by thy great mercy defend us from all perils and dangers of this night; for t' love of Thy only Son our Saviour Jesus Christ."

The office of Compline ended then. But Cedd did not as

usual bless and, as it were, dismiss the monks with the sign of the cross. Instead, he asked them to remain where they stood and, himself standing beside the altar, said, "Brothers, we're surrounded by dangers and darkness. There are all too many men about us who wish us ill, men of little faith and less forgiving." Cedd paused; nobody moved. "Let me speak plainly," he said. "This afternoon, I saw t' Earl Athulf. He argued for his people. He told me they were blaming us for t' wind and rain, t' wrecking of this harvest." He paused again. "Have you heard talk of that?"

A number of the monks nodded and murmured.

"T' Earl says that since they deserted Freya for Christ, they've had more foul days than fine." Cedd threw back his head. "As if an idol could change t' weather," he said contemptuously. "But that's not all. He said we were stripping families of sons against their will. That's not so. He said we were taking food out of t' mouths of his people. But that's not so either; the land we work now was given to us by t' King and not worked before. He said we sheltered wanderers, exiles no other man would give food to or find place for. At times that is so; it's not right that any man under heaven should starve or freeze. And he said that our cows had twice strayed and eaten off the common land. If that is so, we should be more careful." Cedd looked about him. "And lastly t' Earl said that we are accused of moving land markers."

Several monks murmured angrily.

"I'm sure that is not so."

Wulf shook his head fiercely.

30

"I'm sure that is not so," repeated Cedd. He fingered the gleaming cross that hung round his neck. "I answered t' Earl as I've spoken to you. And I told him, too, that we've come here to give, to help, to warn, to love, as Christ commands us; not to take or wrong or damage in any way." Cedd, it seemed, half-smiled. "Brothers," he went on, "t' people have a bad harvest. They fear t' wolf of winter. And they're afraid of our ways, as all men fear what they cannot fully understand. They're angry and unhappy; do not make them more so."

Wulf peered about the church. The monks cast giant blurred shadows on the roof and the walls, as moving clouds do over green fields and fields of corn.

"If you're struck on one cheek, turn t' other," said Cedd.

"Answer bitterness with kindness; be generous to mean-minded men. It's not easy; I never pretended that." He shook his head, and spoke quietly now as a pigeon at nightfall in a silent wood. "Be peaceful. Let time pass and t' anger of those now against us will pass too. Be peaceful this night."

Cedd made the sign of the cross then, and the monks drifted out into the summer night. Wulf walked sedately back to the dormitory, carrying Cedd's words and warnings with him. It took him less time to get to sleep than he expected.

3

The fine weather came too late. The benign sun, the cloudless skies mocked the villagers as they reaped their harvest, such

as it was. Side by side with the monks, they sullenly cut their corn, and their women followed after them, gleaning the ears that survived the gleaming scythes.

Wulf's mother said that every man and woman and child in Ythancestir would go short that winter. "That's our fate," she said. "And one way or another the monks will pay for it," she warned Wulf darkly. "That will be their fate."

After the reaping, the stubble was fired. More than twenty small strips of flame flickered and prospered in the dry last days of summer. Blue smoke wove patterns like rising mist. The sight of it and the thick smell of it filled Wulf with a strong longing, a wonderful ache. At times the smoke thinned until he could only tell it was still in the air because the land behind it—the huts and the forest—seemed to tremble. Then heaven swallowed the smoke.

Wulf was out on the edge of the monastery land, alone with the cattle, when he saw it happen. It happened at the end of a smouldering afternoon when all the monks were in the church arguing (not for the first time) over how the date of Easter should be fixed. It happened so suddenly.

Wulf saw a figure running from the plot of land nearest to the monastery, carrying a burning bundle of rubble, running towards the monastery. It was only two hundred yards. He was there, he was holding up the flickering flames to the thatched roof of the nearest hut, the infirmary.

Wulf was on his feet and shouting and tearing towards the church. "Stop!" he yelled. "Stop! Stop!"

It was already too late. No one and nothing could have

saved the wooden huts with their straw roofs from the greedy tongues of flame. Wulf threw open the doors of the church, still shouting, and the monks streamed out. But the infirmary was already raging; it was a terrifying throat of fire, crackling and spitting, unapproachable.

Then Cedd gave orders—order after order, clearly and firmly. The monks ran to the refectory, the kitchen, the dormitory, the library, the scriptorium, the sculptorium, and came staggering back with whatever they could carry—books, clothing, skins, drinking horns, bellows, half-carved wood and bone and stone, silver ware, tablets of wax. They placed them all in the cool sanctuary of the stone church, and then they turned again and, in twos and threes, coughing and spitting the acrid smoke out of their lungs, they carried out chests and pallets and trestle tables wherever the fire and smoke did not already prevent them. Like a tide the flames flowed from building to building, withering in seconds and minutes what had taken months and years to grow.

When it was no longer possible to withstand the heat and there was nothing more the monks could do, several of them buried their smudged faces in their hands, unable to look, or look at each other, or speak. Only Wulf stood quite apart, knowing and desperate. He kept glancing at the other monks, feeling as guilty and secretive as some thief; there were hammers in his head and chest. He watched roof-beams crack and collapse, and whole walls fall flat, and heard the angry spitting and the voice of the fire. The light wind fanned the flames, leading them first in one direction, then in another. That was

a terrible sight.

Then Cedd asked all the monks to go into the church. Sooty and shaken, but all of them alive and unscathed, they filed slowly into that silent lofty place. Flames lapped around the outside of the stone apse; they could not unmake it.

Cedd himself walked over to Wulf. He knew him so well that, the moment he saw how he looked and behaved, he could tell what had happened. He put an arm round Wulf's shoulders. They stood like that for a moment, the two of them, comforting each other, it seemed; as once they had stood together there, before even the church had been built, sharing a dream. Then Cedd looked earnestly at Wulf and Wulf, his eyes burning with shame, bowed his head. "Yes," he said in a low voice.

Cedd closed his eyes.

Wulf looked at him.

"Aye," said Cedd slowly, and very sadly.

"Oh Cedd!" said Wulf, and suddenly he felt tearful. He screwed up his eyes and rubbed his eyelids.

"Thou'rt sure," said Cedd.

Wulf said, "I saw him."

"T' waste," cried Cedd angrily. "T' waste." Then he took a deep breath and thought for a while. "I've a charge for thee, Wulf," he said at length. "What's worse? To have everything except love? Or to have love but nothing else?"

"We, we . . ." stammered Wulf. "You've often taught us to love, above all to love."

"That is so," said Cedd. "What we've lost we must rebuild; anything man makes can be remade. But thou hast not lost thy love, and thou must not lose it. I know thou dost love him, though you do not think so now. Go to him, comfort him wherever he is."

"I can't," said Wulf in a strangled voice.

"He'll not come back to t' village otherwise. How could he, fearing vengeance as he will? Find him, or he'll be an exile, a wanderer from where to where for as long as he lives."

Wulf looked afraid.

"Tell him our ways are not his ways. Tell him there'll be nowt to answer for, no one to answer to except himself. We've no feuds here."

"He won't understand."

"That's thy charge," said Cedd. "Help him to understand. Go while t' sun is still high."

Wulf ran the whole way to Ythancestir. His long strides ate
up the sandy track. He thought of himself running, he felt the
pounding of his feet, he sidestepped, jumped over potholes,
gasped for air, all he thought of was running for fear of what
lay behind him, and what lay ahead.

Wulf went first to his mother's hut. She was sitting outside
it in the sunlight, plucking a chicken. Anna was making a
maze beside her.

"Oswald," gasped Wulf. "Is he here?"

"Uh?" grunted his mother.

"Oswald. Where is he?"

"I don't know." She shrugged her shoulders. "Why?"

"You haven't seen him?"

"No. Why?"

Wulf looked into the dark hut; it was empty. "The monastery, the whole monastery's burnt," he said, and pointed to the eastern skyline where a great column of smoke was spreading out and feathering. "And, and, well, I think Oswald fired it."

Wulf's mother looked seriously at her younger son; then she averted her gaze from him.

"What?" said Anna. "What did Oswald do?"

"He did," said Wulf. "I saw him."

"No," said Wulf's mother, but Wulf could hear well enough not that she disbelieved him, but that she did not want to believe him. "He wouldn't do that," she said. "You. Your brother. Always at each other. He wouldn't. How could you say that?"

"I saw him," Wulf repeated.

"What did Oswald do?" asked Anna again.

Wulf smiled forlornly at her, and ran one hand through her hair. "I must find him," he said. As he ran off he heard his mother calling and calling after him, "Wulf! Wulf! Wulf!"

It was the same at Earl Athulf's hall; no one had seen Oswald since he had left for his plot of land after the meal at midday. The Earl himself listened and told Wulf, "Find him. Let him speak for himself. If what you say is true, he will never step again on his own land; and no one here will shelter him."

"He hasn't harmed you," said Wulf.

"He's one of us," said Earl Athulf. "Our ways differ from your ways; nevertheless, whether we like it or not, we must learn to live peacefully with you."

"My lord," said Wulf. "If Cedd the Bishop and the monks forgive him, you could forgive him too."

Then Wulf turned and left Earl Athulf's enclosure. He wondered where Oswald would have gone first and decided that he must have run on through the scrub and into the trees that came down almost to the water's edge just north from the monastery. And if he wanted to get as far from the place as possible, thought Wulf, he would then have made inland and rejoined the forest track somewhere beyond Ythancestir.

So Wulf took that track that led westward towards Colchester, wishing he did not have to go into the forest with no hope at all of getting through it before nightfall. He did not run now, there was no point in that. And as he went, he thought of what Cedd might have said to the monks in the church; of how the monks would be scavenging in the ashes for their small precious possessions; how the cattle, the slow, dependable, comforting cows would still have to be milked, fire or no fire. But mostly Wulf thought not back but forward: of how he wanted to find Oswald; how he might have nothing to say when he did meet him; how once, and not since then, they had together taken this same track, hurrying to the great ship-burial at Sutton Hoo. He thought of the dream-dragon in the forest.

The sun dropped and the shadows of the trees grew longer and darker. The shapes of the tree trunks did not reassure Wulf; he didn't want to look at them, and he didn't want not to look at them in case one of them did move and jump as so many of them threatened to do.

It was almost night when Wulf saw ahead of him a little fire by the track side. At once he left the path for the trees and padded through the soft leaf-mould, nearer and nearer to the fire, and the figure sitting beside it. He peered. He inched closer, and peered again, anxious that even a breaking twig might give his presence away. The man was cutting up meat, too attentive to that to notice anything else.

Wulf peered again. He was close enough now; he was sure. "Oswald!" he called in a loud, clear voice.

Oswald leaped to his feet, his knife in his hand.

"Oswald, it's me, it's only me."

"Go away!" said Oswald, his teeth clenched.

"No," said Wulf, and he boldly stepped into the small pool of light surrounding the fire.

"Who's here? Who's with you?"

"No one." Wulf spread out his arms. "Look! I'm alone."

Oswald stared into the almost-darkness behind Wulf.

"I'm hungry too," said Wulf.

Oswald stepped towards the trees with his knife. Nothing moved. He turned back towards Wulf who had dropped on one knee beside the fire, and was staring into it.

A large bird got up near by and Oswald was on his guard again. It flapped heavily away, leaving the two of them to the night-silence.

"Why?" said Wulf. "Oswald, why did you do it?"

"Everyone hates the monks," said Oswald bitterly. "I did what everyone wants to do."

"It's in your own mind," said Wulf sadly. "Partly it is. It's

not like that." He thought for a while; Cedd's words about love came back into his mind, and he was filled with a great relief at having found Oswald. "All the monastery's burned," he said, "all except the church." Then without reproach, he sadly described to Oswald, as if he were his dearest friend, all that had happened—how the monks had lost the buildings it had taken the best part of two years to erect, and lost many more of their possessions than they had been able to save— and Oswald seemed ready enough just to sit and listen.

"So why did you come?" he asked Wulf.

"I don't know," said Wulf, artlessly. "We're brothers, aren't we?"

"I don't understand you."

"Perhaps you don't," said Wulf.

"They'll be after me in the morning," Oswald said.

"No."

"They will. They'll want vengeance."

"No," said Wulf again. "They won't."

"I know how things are. A man who destroys another's property is an outcast always. Before morning I must leave Ythancestir far behind me."

"No," said Wulf a third time, his voice rising.

"I must hunt for the hall of a generous gold-giver," Oswald said, "in some place where no one knows my history."

Wulf shook his head. "Your way is not the way of exile."

"I know how things are," said Oswald fiercely.

"You know how things are between king and earl, earl and freeman," said Wulf urgently, utterly aware that he had a

mission in which he must not fail, and that somehow he must find the right words, the right arguments and answers. "That's not how things are between monks."

"If the monks had never come to Ythancestir, this would never have happened," retorted Oswald.

"The monks want you to come back."

"Come back?" echoed Oswald.

"Come back, to the home where you were born, to the place where you belong. Cedd said so. And the Earl said that we must learn to live together."

"No," said Oswald.

"This is how the Christians are. They're not wonderful but they want no vengeance. They're sad, and they're angry, I think. But they want no part of any feud. If you come back, there'll be no feud, no bitterness. I give you my word."

Oswald sat motionless.

Wulf went on quickly. "Think of our mother and Anna. What could they do without you? Please. And what of the land? Who would work it?"

"I don't know," said Oswald.

"I know you don't like the Christians, but at least their world is kind and forgiving and hopeful. I know you don't like me since . . ."

"It's nothing against you," said Oswald.

"If you were to come, we'd be a kind of cornerstone," said Wulf. "They could all build around us . . ."

"Oh! Your dreams! Your promises!" scoffed Oswald. Despite himself, despite everything, he suddenly grinned and half

embarrassed, he punched Wulf in the ribs as he so often used to do when they were both younger, two brothers under one roof.

"Well," said Wulf excitedly, "so what?"

"You were always like that," said Oswald.

"You'll come," said Wulf. "You'll come now, won't you?"

"I'm hungry," said Oswald. So together they cooked the chunks of meat that he had been preparing when Wulf had first seen him, and then they eagerly devoured them.

"Will we go now?" said Wulf anxiously, feeling that in some strange way he could not control, his brother was already drifting away from him once more.

Oswald shook his head.

"Why not? Why?"

"I don't know," said Oswald stonily. "I want to think."

"Come now," said Wulf.

Again Oswald shook his head.

Then Wulf stood up, and stretched. For a moment he bore down on Oswald's shoulders with both hands. "You will come," he said. "I know you'll come."

Wulf stepped out of the fire circle then, and away into the darkness. He was heading back east. He had done all he could and he believed it might be enough. He suddenly felt so tired, terribly tired, and he wanted to be back with Cedd and the monks. Despite his blood-knot with his mother and Anna and Oswald, he knew that it was with the monks that he could use his talents and find comfort and strength, with the monks that he belonged.

Presently the forest opened, and receded, and only the sleepers of Ythancestir and the sleeping monks lay ahead, the gutted monastery and, beyond, the rocking restless sea.

Wulf heard himself chanting a line from the psalm. "In the habitation of dragons, where each lay, shall be grass with reeds and rushes." He was dazed with effort and tiredness, and couldn't think why the words should have come into his mind.

Just then, and it seemed to Wulf quite wonderful, the great church bell began to toll. Nocturns, he thought. The clear note was a distant voice, a promise.

Wulf hurried through the silent hamlet. And Oswald, he too probably crept back to his place there later that same night.

NOTE

Cedd (pronounced "Ched") began his missionary work amongst the East Saxons in 653. In 656 King Æthelwald granted him land to build a monastery at Ythancestir (pronounced "Oothanchester") which is the present-day Bradwell-on-Sea in Essex. Cedd constructed his church from the remains of the Roman fort of Othona, and brought monks to the monastery south from his native Northumbria. And this church, St Peter-on-the-Wall, perhaps the oldest church in England of which so much remains, still stands for all to see, a great fist surrounded by screaming seabirds, mists, saltmarshes, the sea.

The monks' daily Celebration of the Divine Office consisted of seven services: Matins, Prime, Tierce, Sext, Nones, Vespers and Compline. The midnight service was Nocturns.

The action of this story takes place in the summer of 657, a little more than a year after the building of the church and monastery.